D0606292

Calvin's Christmas Wish

Calvin Miles · Illustrated by Dolores Johnson

Viking

VIKING
Published by the Penguin Group
Penguin Books USA Inc., 375 Hudson Street, New York, New York 10014, U.S.A.
Penguin Books Ltd, 27 Wrights Lane, London W8 5TZ, England
Penguin Books Australia Ltd, Ringwood, Victoria, Australia
Penguin Books Canada Ltd, 10 Alcorn Avenue, Toronto, Ontario, Canada M4V 3B2
Penguin Books (N.Z.) Ltd, 182–190 Wairau Road, Auckland 10, New Zealand

Penguin Books Ltd, Registered Offices: Harmondsworth, Middlesex, England

First published in 1993 by Viking, a division of Penguin Books USA Inc.

1 3 5 7 9 10 8 6 4 2

Library of Congress Catalog Card Number: 93-60591 ISBN 0-670-84295-8
Printed in Hong Kong Set in 14 point Clarendon Light

To Courtney

—C. M.

To all my cousins

—D. J.

I remember my favorite gift from Santa Claus. Maybe I remember it so well because I was so worried about it. . . .

On the last day of school before Christmas vacation, I was walking home with my friends W.C. and Earl. We were talking about what we wanted for Christmas. I told them that Santa Claus was going to bring me a bike.

W.C. laughed. "Ain't no such thing as Santa Claus."

"How you know?" I asked.

"Your parents is Santa Claus," he said. "I saw my ma hidin' gifts under the bed."

I said good-bye to W.C. and Earl, and as I turned up the road, I felt terrible. I thought, how could what W.C. said be true? I knew my Momma bought us clothes for Christmas, but I never saw her getting any toys for us. And last year I hadn't seen the doll baby my little sister got, or my tin wagon, until Christmas morning. Our house was so small—how could Momma have hidden all those toys?

I said to myself, "W.C.'s just jealous 'cause I'm getting a brand-new bike for Christmas." At least I hoped I was.

When I got home, I decided not to tell my sisters or my brother I was worried. I didn't want anyone to know. I just wanted a bike so bad. Earl had a Hopalong Cassidy model and it was the most perfect bike I had ever seen. He wouldn't let me ride it, but he would ride me on the back. If there was no Santa Claus, I wouldn't get my bike for Christmas!

When I went inside, Momma was in the kitchen, making pies and humming a Christmas carol. I thought about how each year she saved money to buy us all new clothes. She had to make a special trip to town to buy them, and sometimes I went with her. You knew it was near Christmas because the store in our town put up lots of decorations. And there were all kinds of fruit to buy that you didn't see during the hot months: oranges, apples, tangerines—and lots of candy canes and chocolate Santas.

I watched Momma cooking and smelled the apple pies she was baking for the holidays. I thought, with Momma getting ready for Christmas, how could there *not* be a Santa Claus? I asked Momma again, to be sure.

"Yes, Calvin," she said. "There is a Santa Claus."

That didn't stop me worrying, though. What if W.C. was right? If my parents *were* Santa Claus, they couldn't afford special presents. We didn't have much money this year. And the bike I saw in the Sears catalog cost an awful lot. Santa was my only hope of getting that bike.

On the day before Christmas, Momma told me and my little sister Thelma to go get a Christmas tree. We went to the woods to find the perfect one. In North Carolina, it doesn't usually snow at Christmastime. But everything in the woods seems brighter.

Some Christmases we couldn't find just the right tree, no matter how long we looked. We liked them without any spaces between the branches. Some years we had to put two trees together to make it look good. But this time we were lucky. We found just the right tree on the edge of the woods. I thought finding the perfect tree was a good sign. So didn't that mean that Santa would have to come?

On the way home, Thelma gathered pinecones. She said that Santa Claus was bringing her a tea set for Christmas. I asked her, "How do you know that Santa is going to bring you what you want?"

"I wrote him a letter," Thelma answered. "I told Santa to bring me a beautiful tea set." And that seemed to settle it for her. But she was just a little girl. She didn't know that there might not be a Santa Claus.

Still, for Thelma's sake, I pretended to be sure that Santa would come. "I'm getting a bike for Christmas. I showed Ma in the catalog the kind of bike I want, and Ma said Daddy would tell Santa to bring it."

I'd been carrying the tree while we talked, but now it was getting very heavy. "Let me carry the ax, Thelma," I said. "You might get cut."

"I know how to hold an ax, and I'm not carrying that tree!" Thelma answered. That was the end of that.

When we got back, Momma was at the kitchen table cutting out paper stars. Thelma put the pinecones on the table beside them. Daddy would put the tree up in the living room later. Our sisters, Earlene and Lillian, were helping Momma. They painted the stars white, yellow, and silver. They painted the pinecones blue, red, yellow, and white.

Momma sent me to help put up the decorations outside the house. My older brother, Marshall, and I put holly branches all around the front porch. We hung the wreath we made on the front door.

Then came my favorite part: I put decorations around the barn where the animals were. Daddy helped me. We didn't put up much, just enough to let the animals know it was holiday time. I looked at the pigs and the chickens, the cow and mules—they were so happy. They didn't have to work in the fields, because it was Christmas. And they didn't worry about Santa at all.

That night, when all the decorations were made, everyone in the family hung them on the tree. We didn't have electricity, but in the glow of the kerosene lamps, the silver stars on the tree seemed to twinkle.

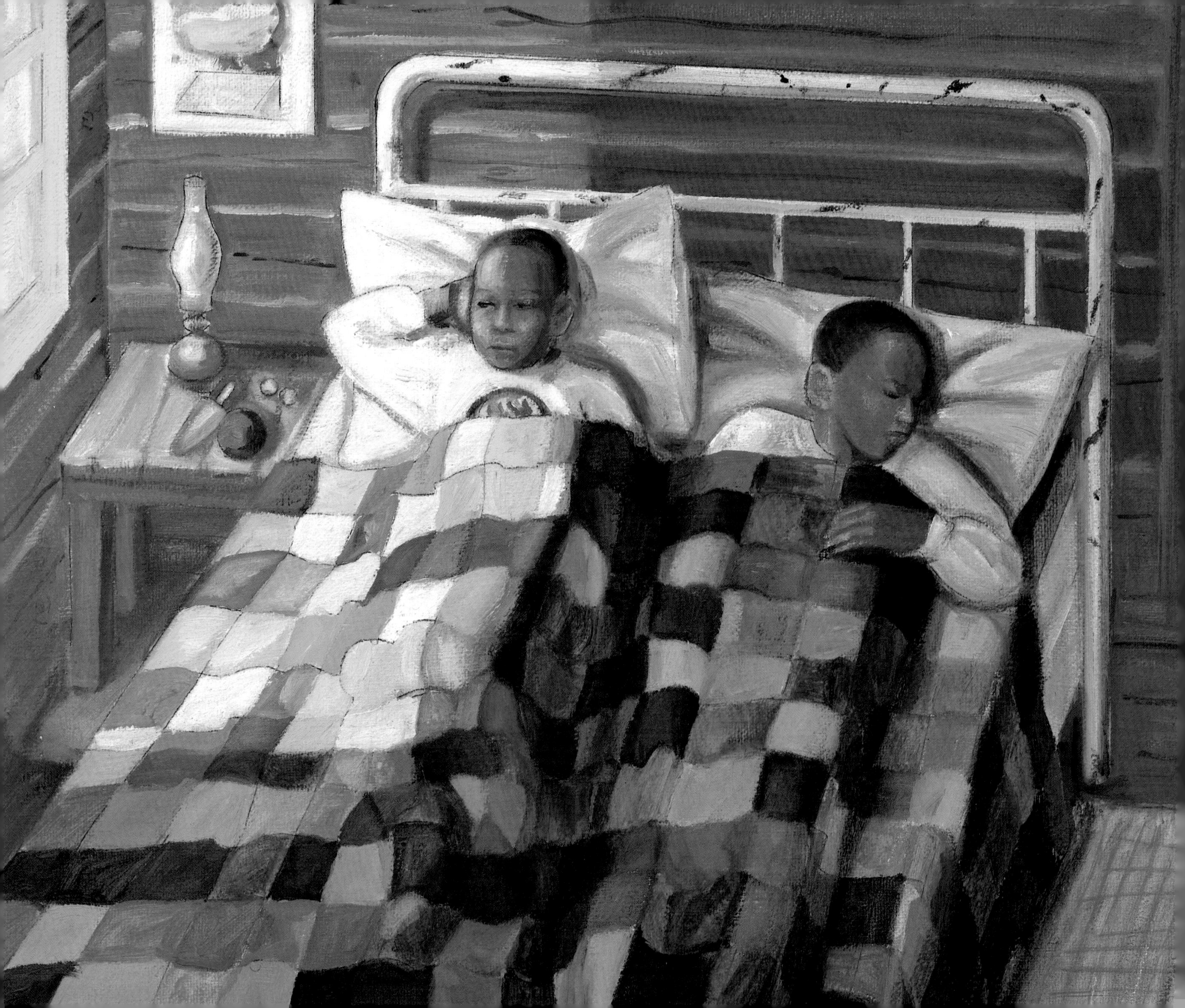

Later, it was hard to sleep. I lay in bed, listening for any noise that might be Santa. I heard something moving—was that him? I finally went to sleep, but I woke up very early. I lay in bed watching the sky get light and wondering if Santa Claus had come. I told myself to act excited even if he *hadn't* come, so that no one would know I was disappointed. At least there would be the special boxes for each of us that Momma made every year. They would be filled with apples and pecans, and the oranges I loved so much. I would get new clothes too. But in my heart, I still wanted that bike.

Finally Daddy called us. It was all right to come see what we got for Christmas. I jumped out of bed.

Then I saw it, right from the door of our room. A shiny green bike next to the Christmas tree! I ran over to it, my heart pounding. It was perfect! It had a horn and a bell and streamers and a mirror. My bike had *everything*. Santa had come after all.

I raced to get dressed. The whole family ate breakfast together, and we looked at each other's presents. Thelma had her new tea set, and everyone showed off their new clothes. But I couldn't wait to get on that bike. As soon as breakfast was over, I hopped right on and rode it over to Earl's house. Then Earl and I left for W.C.'s. I couldn't wait to show him that Santa had come and brought me what I wanted most of all.

Author's Note

Calvin's Christmas Wish is the story of a very special Christmas for me. I began this story in a writing group at Literacy Volunteers of New York City. I was thirty-nine years old at the time and I was learning to read and write.

When I was young, I lived on a farm in North Carolina, just like in this book. I went to school for a few years, but when I got older, my family needed me to work on the farm. As a young man, I moved to New York City. I worked hard and raised two sons. When they were grown, I decided to go back to school to learn to read and write.

At Literacy Volunteers, I studied with a group of adults like myself. One night, we decided we would each write about Christmas. Memories of my childhood came back to me. When I read my story to the group, they asked me questions that brought back even more details.

The editors at Literacy Volunteers of New York City saw my story and liked it. They wanted to make my story into a book for adults who are learning to read. The book, *When Dreams Came True*, was published in paperback and illustrated with photographs. I was glad my book could help other adults learn to read.

The editors at Viking Children's Books saw *When Dreams Came True* and asked me to work on the story again. It became the children's book you are reading. Having my story made into a book for children is important to me because I now have a two-year-old granddaughter, Courtney Miles, to read it with.

I would like to thank my writing group for their encouragement. I would also like to thank Sarah Kirshner, Elizabeth Law, Nancy McCord, Marie Magno, Ed Susse, and Eli Zal, with special thanks to Lynne Sherman. Finally, I would like to thank Literacy Volunteers of New York City for making my dreams come true in many ways.